RENATA, WHIZBRAIN AND THE GHOST

by Caron Lee Cohen

illustrated by Blanche Sims

Atheneum *1987* *New York*

For Margaret Gabel
(C.L.C.)

To Loretta, Greg, Debbie, and Billy, with love
(B.S.)

Atheneum
Macmillan Publishing Company
866 Third Avenue, New York, NY 10022

Type set by Linoprint Composition Co., Inc., New York City
Printed and bound by The South China Printing Company, Hong Kong
Typography by Mary Ahern
First Edition

10 9 8 7 6 5 4 3 2 1

Library of Congress Cataloging in Publication Data

Cohen, Caron Lee.
Renata, Whizbrain, and the ghost.

SUMMARY: Relates how Red River Renata and Whizbrain
Wallerbee use his invention, the ice box railroad car,
to retrieve the sunken treasure jealously guarded by the
ghost of Fearless Bones Kelly.
[1. Buried treasure—Fiction. 2. Ghosts—Fiction.
3. Tall tales. 4. Humorous stories] I. Sims, Blanche,
ill. II. title.
PZ7.C6574Re 1987 [E] 86-22330
ISBN 0-689-31271-7

IN OLD TIME Texas everyone knew about the sunken treasure of the Red River. Everyone wanted it too. There was one hitch. It was haunted! That treasure was haunted by the ghost of Fearless Bones Kelly.

When Fearless Bones was still alive, he was a river pirate. He was famous for two things—being greedy and cursing.

The day he died, he was sailing the Red River with a treasure chest full of loot when his boat began to sink. He could have swum ashore, but he was too greedy to leave his treasure. He was madder than a wet hen! "Goldang it!" he cursed. And then he drowned.

The ghost of Fearless Bones Kelly was like no other. He was chock full of river water! On land, he was a walking flood. He splashed, and he gushed, and he drenched every doggone thing.

A ghost needs a treasure as much as a dog needs two tails. But Fearless Bones was just as greedy dead as he was alive! He would never let that treasure out of his sight.

ROOMS
STORE
HAIR EMPORIUM

Lots of folks went out to the Red River and hauled up the chest. They took it home, but there was Fearless Bones. "Darn! Dang! Drat!" he'd curse. And he'd drench everything. No one wanted that treasure enough to put up with a flood. So those folks just threw it back in the Red River.

Now Red River Renata worked morning, noon, and night in Amarillo City Hall. She was mayor, sheriff, fire marshal, postmaster, and patent agent. She always figured there must be a way to get that treasure without drowning in a flood. She just couldn't think of the way.

TOWN
MAYOR
SHERIFF
POST OFFICE

AMARILLO
CITY HALL

Well, on November 26, 1867, Whizbrain Wallerbee walked into Amarillo City Hall. He asked to see the patent agent.

That changed everything.

"Howdy, ma'am," said Whizbrain. "I'd like a patent for my invention—the Ice Box Car."

"What's that?" asked Renata.

"It's a railroad car folks can fill up with ice," said Whizbrain. "Why, take a Fort Worth & Denver Railroad car. Fill 'er up with Rocky Mountain ice in Denver. Carry it all the way to Fort Worth. That's seven hundred miles!"

"You mean," said Renata, "you could get me real ice, here in Amarillo?"

"That's right,"said Whizbrain. "And just as fast as you can sing 'Oh Suzannah!'" Renata gave Whizbrain patent number 71423. Then she got thinking. After a moment she whispered a plan to him.

"It's a deal," he said.

$500.
REWARD

Then Whizbrain filled up an ice box car in Denver, hitched it to a train, unhitched it in Amarillo and hauled it out onto a flatboat in the Red River. He did all that faster than Renata could sing "Oh Suzannah!"

ICE

SAND
SAND
SAND

Then he got one hook,
six feet of chain,
six bags of sand,
six pairs of long underwear,
six fur coats,
two raincoats,
two pairs of rubbers,
two pairs of mittens,
and two rain hats.
He put them on the deck
of that flatboat.
That took a little longer.

Then Whizbrain and Renata sailed out on the Red River. They fished around for the treasure. When they found it, they dragged it up with their hook and chain.

Then up jumped Fearless Bones. He started right off cursing, "Goldarn and …"

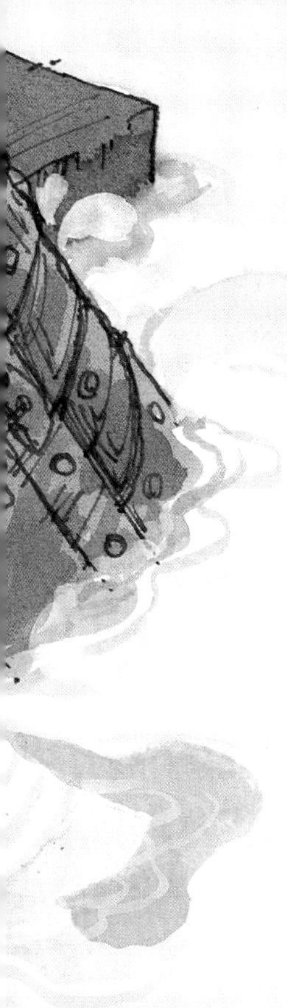

But before he could say, "thunderation," Whizbrain and Renata were all dressed and ready. They each put on three pairs of long underwear, three fur coats, one raincoat, one pair of rubbers, one pair of mittens, and one rain hat.

Then Fearless Bones started flooding every doggone thing. But Renata and Whizbrain just picked up that treasure chest and carried it into the ice box car.

Kelly said, "Goldang, you two. You'll never get my treasure!" He followed them into the ice box car.

Whizbrain and Renata sat down and waited. Kelly splashed, and he gushed, and he watched that water just freeze on the floor!

"Well, kiss my bones!" he said.

Then Kelly began to shiver. "Darn cold in here," he said. First his toes froze. Then his nose froze. Then his arms and legs froze.

Whizbrain and Renata just sat in all their clothes as warm and dry as two slices of toast. They began to sing, "Oh, Suzannah, don't you cry for me. . . ."

But Fearless Bones was crying icicles! Soon he was stiffer than a fish in a block of ice. He couldn't splash. He couldn't gush. He couldn't drench a doggone thing. He was frozen solid!

Renata and Whizbrain walked out on the deck with the treasure chest. They took out the gold and filled the chest with sand. Then they put the chest back next to Fearless Bones.

Renata and Whizbrain jumped for joy.

"Whoopee, yippee," they cried. "We are rich!"

SAND

When the ice box car finally thawed, so did the ghost of Fearless Bones Kelly.

"Darn cold winter we had," he said.

Then he just took his chest and jumped into the Red River. He needed that loot like a dog needs two tails, so he never opened the chest to find out it was filled with sand.

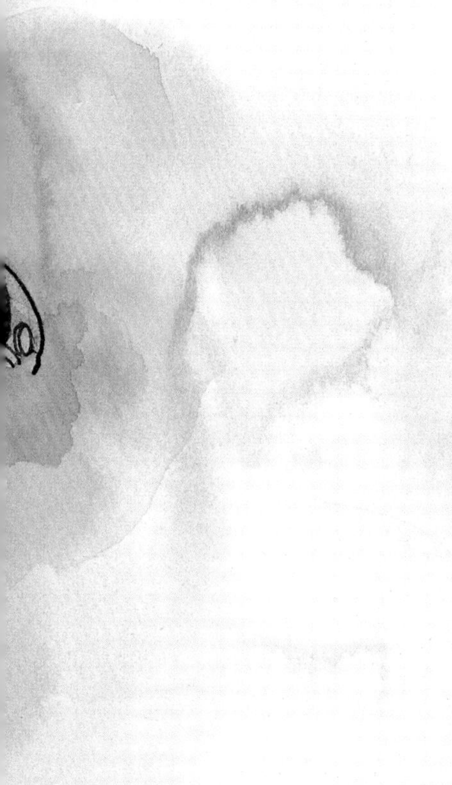

Renata and Whizbrain lived high on the hog in Amarillo for the rest of their lives. But they weren't greedy.

They shared that gold with all the folks who lived for miles around.